FRANZ BRANDENBERG

IT'S NOT MY FAULT

illustrated by ALIKI

GREENWILLOW BOOKS
New York

A Division of William Morrow & Company, Inc., 105 Madison Avenue, New York, N.Y. 10016
Printed in the United States of America   First Edition   10 9 8 7 6 5 4 3 2

Library of Congress Cataloging in Publication Data
Brandenberg, Franz.   It's not my fault   (Greenwillow read-alone books)
Summary: The Fieldmouse family have one of those days when everyone
quarrels with everyone else until a pot of soup is peacemaker.
[1. Mice—Fiction.   2. Family life—Fiction]   I. Aliki.   II. Title.
PZ7.B7364It   [E]   79-24157   ISBN 0-688-80235-4   ISBN 0-688-84235-6 lib. bdg.

FOR SUSAN

CONTENTS

PROLOGUE

"No fighting today, children, please!"
said Mother Fieldmouse.

"It isn't my fault," said Annette.

"If only the others left me alone!"
said Bertrand.

"I always get the blame," said Colette.

"I never start it," said Daniel.

"Everybody interferes,"
     said Esther.

"They always pick on me!"
     said Ferdinand.

"I guess it's going to be
one of those days,"
said Father Fieldmouse.

CHAPTER 1

Bertrand was building a tower.

"Can we help you?" asked Annette.

"No, thank you," replied Bertrand.

"The blocks don't belong to you,"
  said Colette.

"But I had them first," said Bertrand.

"Selfish!" said Esther.

"Leave me alone!" said Bertrand.

Daniel knocked the tower down.

"You are mean!" cried Bertrand.

"So are you," said Ferdinand.

"I wish I didn't have

any brothers and sisters!"

said Bertrand.

"I think you need
a vacation from each other,"
said Mother Fieldmouse.
"Who wants to come
shopping with me?"
asked Father Fieldmouse.
"I!" said Annette, Colette,
Daniel, Esther, and Ferdinand.

yea!

"I want to stay home!"

said Bertrand.

"Good for us!"

said his brothers and sisters.

"I hope you never come back!"

said Bertrand.

Bertrand had the blocks
all to himself.
He built a store
with a counter and shelves,
and put things on them.

He waited and waited.

But nobody came.

"What good is a store

with no customers?"

he said to himself.

He knocked the store down.

Bertrand put on his crown.

He built a castle,

and sat in it.

"Can you see me?"

he shouted.

No one answered.

"What good is a castle

if nobody knows

that I am in it?"

he said to himself.

He knocked the castle down.

He built a tower.

"Come see how high it is!"
he shouted.

No one answered.

"What good is a tower
if there is nobody to admire it?"
he said to himself.

He knocked the tower down.

"It's not even fun
to knock it down
if nobody gets mad,"
he said to himself.

Just then his father and brothers
and sisters came home.

"How did you get along
without us?" asked Annette.

"I had the blocks
all to myself," said Bertrand.

"Was it fun?" asked Colette.

"No," replied Bertrand.

"Do you want to build a store?"

"Yes, let's!" they all said.

They built a store
with a counter and shelves,
and put things on them.
"I am the storekeeper,
and you are the customers,"
said Bertrand.

"No!" said Esther.

"We want to be storekeepers, too."

"Then let's take turns,"

said Bertrand.

Everyone got a turn

at being the storekeeper.

STEP
RIGHT
UP!

"Do you want to build a castle?"
asked Bertrand.
"Yes, let's!" they all said.
They built a castle.
"I get to sit in it,
because I am the king,"
said Bertrand.
"No!" said Daniel.
"We want to sit in it, too."

"Then let's take turns,"
said Bertrand.
Everyone got a turn
at wearing the crown
and sitting in the castle.

"Do you want to build a tower?"
asked Bertrand.

"Yes, let's!" they all said.

They built a tower.

"I want to knock it down,"
  said Ferdinand.

"Then I'll get mad,"
  said Bertrand.

"You are supposed to,"
  said Ferdinand.

"That's the fun of it."

"You are right," said Bertrand.

"Who would you get mad at
  if you didn't have us?"
  said Annette.

"Brothers and sisters
  are good for something after all,"
  said Bertrand.

Everyone helped knock the tower down.
They all had fun, and no one got mad.

"You have worked hard,"
said Father Fieldmouse.
"You must be hungry."
"We are!" replied
all the Fieldmouse children.

CHAPTER 2

"What kind of soup would you like?"
asked Mother Fieldmouse.

"Carrot soup, please," said Annette.

"Onion soup, please," said Bertrand.

"Green soup, please," said Colette.

"Tomato soup, please," said Daniel.

"Beet soup, please," said Esther.

"Bread soup, please," said Ferdinand.

"Very well,"

said Mother Fieldmouse.

"Get to work."

Annette grated the carrots.

Bertrand chopped the onions.

Colette cut the greens.

Daniel quartered the tomatoes.

Esther sliced the beets.

Ferdinand diced the bread.

"We are done," said Annette.

"What do we do next?" asked Esther.

"Everyone gets a pot,"
   said Father Fieldmouse.

"We don't have six pots,"
   said Mother Fieldmouse.

"Oh, no!"
   said the Fieldmouse children.

"What are we going to do with
all this food?" asked Colette.
"Let's put it all in one pot,"
said Father Fieldmouse.
"Yea!"
said the Fieldmouse children.

Father Fieldmouse filled the pot

with water and put it on the stove.

Annette added the grated carrots.

Bertrand added the chopped onions.

Colette added the cut greens.

Daniel added the quartered tomatoes.

Esther added the sliced beets.

Ferdinand added the diced bread.

And Mother Fieldmouse

added the salt.

41

wait for me!

"This is going to be

the best soup ever,"

said Father Fieldmouse.

"Because of the carrots," said Annette.

"Because of the onions," said Bertrand.

"Because of the greens," said Colette.

"Because of the tomatoes," said Daniel.

"Because of the beets," said Esther.

"Because of the bread," said Ferdinand.

"We'll soon find out,"

said Mother Fieldmouse.

"It's ready!

To the table every one!"

CHAPTER 3

"The best soup ever!"

said the Fieldmouse children.

"Let's enjoy it in peace,"

said Father Fieldmouse.

"No talking for a while!"

Bertrand poked Annette.

Annette poked Bertrand.

Bertrand poked Annette.

Annette spilled her soup.

"Annette! Please clean up the soup,"

said Mother Fieldmouse.

"It wasn't my fault,"

said Annette.

"Bertrand poked me."

"Annette poked me, too,"

said Bertrand.

"Bertrand started it," said Annette.

Colette giggled.

"Be quiet, Colette!"

said Mother Fieldmouse.

"You always blame the girls,"

said Colette.

"Please leave the table, Colette!"

said Father Fieldmouse.

Colette left the table.

Daniel clapped his hands.

"That wasn't called for, Daniel,"
said Father Fieldmouse.

"You always blame the boys,"
said Daniel.

"Please leave the table, Daniel!"
said Mother Fieldmouse.

Daniel left the table.

"Mother always interferes,"
said Esther.
"Please leave the table, Esther!"
said Father Fieldmouse.
Esther left the table.

"Bravo!" said Ferdinand.

"That wasn't necessary, Ferdinand,"
 said Father Fieldmouse.

"You always pick on me,"
 said Ferdinand.

"Please leave the table, Ferdinand!"
 said Mother Fieldmouse.

Ferdinand left the table.

"Haven't you two
cleaned up
the spilled soup yet?"
asked Father Fieldmouse.
"It wasn't my fault,"
said Annette.
"I didn't spill it,"
said Bertrand.
"Please, both of you
leave the table!"
said Mother Fieldmouse.

"Who is going to eat

all this soup?"

asked Father Fieldmouse.

"You sent the children away,"

said Mother Fieldmouse.

"So did you,"

said Father Fieldmouse.

"You started it,"

said Mother Fieldmouse.

"Do you want me

to leave the table?"

asked Father Fieldmouse.

"If you do, who is going to eat
all this soup?"
asked Mother Fieldmouse.
They both laughed.

Father got the sponge
and cleaned up
the spilled soup.

"Whoever is hungry
may come back!"
called Mother Fieldmouse.
All the Fieldmouse children
returned to the table.

Annette nudged Bertrand.

Bertrand nudged Colette.

Colette nudged Daniel.

Daniel nudged Esther.

Esther nudged Ferdinand.

Ferdinand almost spilled his soup.

"That's enough!"

said Father Fieldmouse.

Mother Fieldmouse nudged him.

Father Fieldmouse spilled his soup.

"It wasn't my fault!" he said.

They all laughed.

Bertrand got the sponge
and cleaned up the spilled soup.
"Who would like more?"
asked Mother Fieldmouse.
"I!" said Father Fieldmouse
and all the Fieldmouse children.

EPILOGUE

"That was some day,"

  said Mother Fieldmouse.

"It wasn't my fault,"

  said Father Fieldmouse.

"No fighting, please,"

  called the Fieldmouse children.

  Mother and Father Fieldmouse laughed.

"I wonder what tomorrow will bring,"

  said Mother Fieldmouse.

"More soup, I hope,"

  said Father Fieldmouse.

FRANZ and ALIKI BRANDENBERG are
husband and wife. They have collaborated on a
group of books about a family of cats—*A Secret for
Grandmother's Birthday, A Robber! A Robber!,
I Wish I Was Sick, Too!* and *A Picnic, Hurrah!*
—as well as on several books about a Fieldmouse
family, which include *What Can You Make of It?,
Nice New Neighbors, Six New Students,* and *Everyone Ready?* Among their other collaborations arc
Jason and Alexa, their two children.